TRANS FORMERS ™

Transformers: Optimus Prime Versus Megatron
Printed in the United States of America.
All rights reserved. No part of this book may be used or reproduced in any manner whatsoever without written permission except in the case of brief quotations embodied in critical articles and reviews. For information address HarperCollins Children's Books, a division of HarperCollins Publishers, 1350 Avenue of the Americas, New York, NY 10019.
www.harpercollinschildrens.com

Library of Congress catalog card number: 2006935091
ISBN-10: 0-06-088824-5 — ISBN-13: 978-0-06-088824-4
❖
First Edition

TRANSFORMERS ™

OPTIMUS PRIME VERSUS MEGATRON

ADAPTED BY SADIE CHESTERFIELD
ILLUSTRATED BY VAL STAPLES

HarperEntertainment
An Imprint of HarperCollins*Publishers*

not long ago on a planet called Cybertron, members of an alien race battled against each other. They were called the Transformers. Their war left the planet in ruin and forever divided two brothers.

These brothers, known as Optimus Prime and Megatron, became fierce enemies. Megatron set out to conquer the planet. Because of this betrayal, Optimus was forced to battle his brother.

Optimus Prime led the Autobots, a group of Transformers who protected life in all forms. He was a wise leader, and quickly gained the respect of his army.

Megatron proved to be the opposite. He fed on the "Spark," or life force, of the defeated. He led his followers on brutal rampages. These Transformers were known as the Decepticons.

When the war on Cybertron ended, the Transformers who survived were forced to flee. Many came to Earth in search of the Allspark, the supreme power that fills Transformers with the gift of the Spark.

On a roadway near the dam, the Decepticons assembled for the return of their leader. They were ready to seize the Allspark and conquer Earth. But the Autobots could not let that happen.

Arriving on the scene, they prepared to battle the Decepticons as they had on Cybertron. Then Megatron exploded out of the ground. He ripped out the Spark of an Autobot named Jazz. From a hundred feet away, Optimus Prime watched in horror.

Optimus ran toward Megatron, destroying everything in his path. Megatron tried to escape, but Optimus grabbed him and the two brothers crashed to the ground. Megatron stared coldly at Optimus. "Brother, our war begins again . . . on Earth."

Metal fists flew through the air. Transformer fought Transformer.

Sam looked on in amazement. He needed to help his new friends, the Autobots.

In the chaos, he seized the Allspark.

If he could get to higher ground, Sam might be able to escape on a helicopter. Then the Allspark, and Earth, would be safe from the Decepticons.

Suddenly, something exploded through the ground beneath him. It was Megatron!
"Give me the Allspark, boy! You aren't strong enough to defy me!" he yelled.
Megatron fired at Sam, and Sam started to fall.

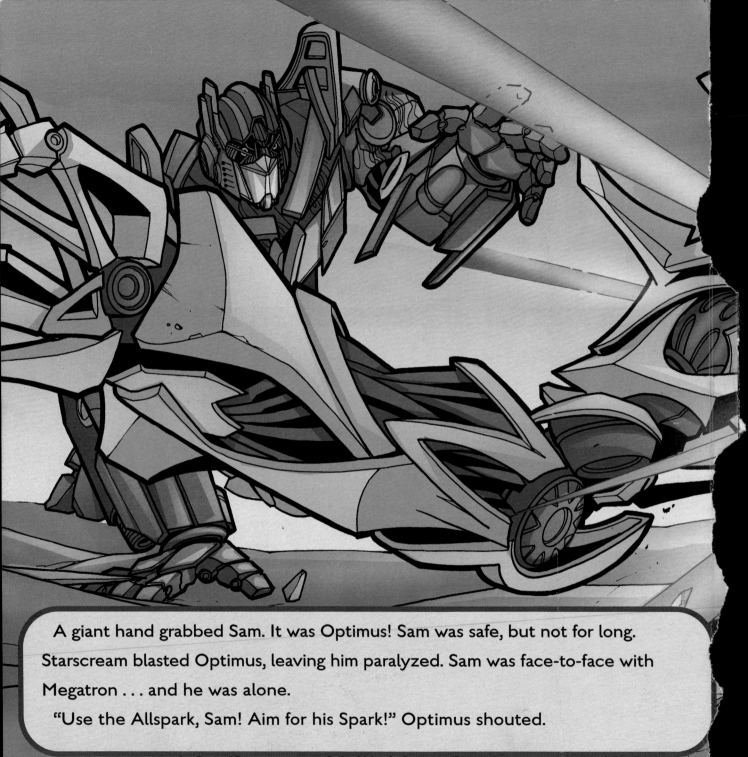

A giant hand grabbed Sam. It was Optimus! Sam was safe, but not for long. Starscream blasted Optimus, leaving him paralyzed. Sam was face-to-face with Megatron . . . and he was alone.

"Use the Allspark, Sam! Aim for his Spark!" Optimus shouted.

Sam did just that. He jammed the Allspark into Megatron's chest. In a blinding flash, Megatron's Spark exploded.

It was all over.

With their leader gone, the last of the Decepticons fled the planet.

A few days later, Optimus watched as Megatron's body was lowered into the ocean. "You left me no choice, brother," he said softly. The Autobots had won. The war was finally over . . . for now.